THE BEST
HOCKEY
PLAYERS
OF ALL TIME

Rockport Public Library
17 School Street
Rockport, MA 01966

By Will Graves

www.abdopublishing.com

Published by Abdo Publishing, a division of ABDO, PO Box 398166, Minneapolis, Minnesota 55439. Copyright © 2015 by Abdo Consulting Group, Inc. International copyrights reserved in all countries. No part of this book may be reproduced in any form without written permission from the publisher. SportsZone™ is a trademark and logo of Abdo Publishing.

Printed in the United States of America, North Mankato, Minnesota
092014
012015

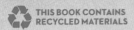
THIS BOOK CONTAINS RECYCLED MATERIALS

Cover Photos: Saxon/AP Images, left; Keith Srakocic/AP Images, right
Interior Photos: Saxon/AP Images, 1 (left); Keith Srakocic/AP Images, 1 (right); AP Images, 7, 9, 11, 17, 19, 21, 25; Bettmann/Corbis, 13; Harry Cabluck/AP Images, 15; A. E. Maloof/AP Images, 23; Bill Kostroun/ AP Images, 27, 51; IHA/Icon SMI, 29; Dave Buston/AP Images, 31; Bourdier/AP Images, 33; Rusty Kennedy/AP Images, 35; Ron Frehm/ AP Images, 37; Fred Jewell/AP Images, 39; Eric Gay/AP Images, 41; Gary Tramontina/AP Images, 43; Gene J. Puskar/AP Images, 45, 47; Jerry S. Mendoza/AP Images, 49; Julie Jacobson/AP Images, 53; Petr David Josek/AP Images, 55; Iurii Osadchi/Shutterstock Images, 57; photosthatrock/Shutterstock Images, 59; Chris O'Meara/AP Images, 61

Editor: Patrick Donnelly
Series Designer: Christa Schneider

Library of Congress Control Number: 2014944193

Cataloging-in-Publication Data
Graves, Will.
 The best hockey players of all time / Will Graves.
   p. cm. -- (Sports' best ever)
ISBN 978-1-62403-620-0 (lib. bdg.)
Includes bibliographical references and index.
1. Hockey--Juvenile literature.   I. Title.
796.962--dc23

                                        2014944193

TABLE OF CONTENTS

INTRODUCTION

Hockey players have a unique set of skills. In many ways, they are not like other athletes.

They skate instead of run. They shoot instead of throw. And they check instead of tackle.

But like other athletes, they are supremely skilled and consistently tough. They rely on stamina and endurance to pass the game's most grueling tests. And the best players get the coolest nicknames: "The Rocket," "Sid the Kid," "The Great One," and "Super Mario."

They all followed different paths to the National Hockey League (NHL). Yet they all had one thing in common. They loved to play the game.

Here are some of the greatest hockey players of all time.

MAURICE RICHARD

The Montreal Canadiens were looking for players. Maurice Richard was looking for a job. And an open tryout provided hockey with its first superstar.

The 21-year-old Richard skated onto the ice. It did not take long for him to catch the attention of his new teammates and earn one of hockey's first great nicknames: "The Rocket."

Montreal veteran Ray Getliffe called Richard "The Rocket" because of how fast he could skate. But Getliffe might as well have been talking about how quickly Richard could score goals. He became the first player in league history to score 50 goals in one season. That was in 1944–45, when the league played just 50 games per year. Two years later he won the Hart Trophy, which is given to the league's most valuable player (MVP).

"The Rocket" scored 50 goals in 50 games in 1944–45.

But Richard could do more than just pump pucks into the net. He was one of the toughest players in the NHL too. One of his most famous goals came in Game 7 of the 1952 Stanley Cup semifinals. Montreal and the Boston Bruins were tied midway through the game when Richard fell face-first onto the ice. He went to the locker room and came back with his face covered in stitches. But he refused to let that slow him down. With blood dripping down his face, Richard scored the winning goal.

Though Montreal did not win the title that year, the Canadiens did capture the Stanley Cup eight times during Richard's career, including five straight from 1956 to 1960. Richard retired after the 1959–60 season with 544 career goals. That was still a team record through 2014.

He came a long way from that open tryout in 1942.

82

The number of career playoff goals Maurice Richard scored. That still ranked eighth in NHL history through 2014.

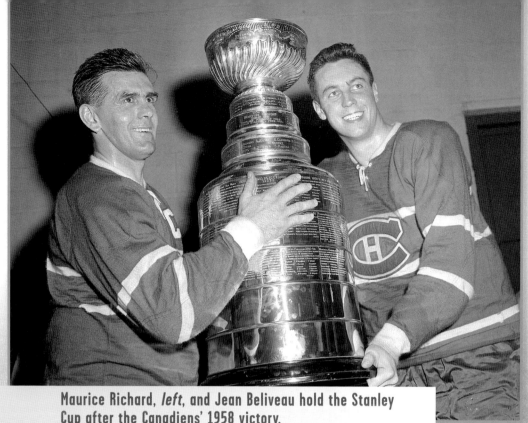

Maurice Richard, *left*, and Jean Beliveau hold the Stanley Cup after the Canadiens' 1958 victory.

MAURICE RICHARD

Hometown: Montreal, Quebec, Canada

Height, Weight: 5 feet 10, 170 pounds

Birth Date: August 4, 1921

Position: Right wing

Team: Montreal Canadiens (1942–60)

NHL All-Star Games: 13 (1947–59)

Hart Trophy (NHL MVP): 1 (1946–47)

All-NHL First Team: 8 (1944–45 through 1949–50, 1954–55, 1955–56)

GORDIE HOWE

Gordie Howe played his first NHL game on October 16, 1946. He was just 18 years old. All he wanted to do was hang on to his roster spot.

The man nicknamed "Mr. Hockey" did more than that. He scored a goal in his first game for the Detroit Red Wings. Then he added 800 more goals during an NHL career that lasted 25 years. At the age of 43, Howe retired from the Red Wings but not from the sport he loved.

After taking two years off, he returned in 1973 to play in the new World Hockey Association (WHA). He joined his sons Mark and Marty on the ice with the Houston Aeros and the New England Whalers. Howe played in the WHA for six seasons, but the league folded in 1979. At age 51, Howe played his last season back in the NHL.

Gordie Howe played in the NHL in five different decades.

Wherever Howe played, he scored.

While he never led the NHL in goals, he always seemed to be near the top of the list. He finished in the top five in scoring for 20 straight years, which is a mark that might never be broken.

Howe did more than shoot the puck at the net. He also helped make professional hockey popular in the United States. When he joined the NHL, there were just six teams in the league. By the time he retired in 1980, there were 21 teams spread out across North America.

1,767

The number of games Gordie Howe played in during his NHL career, a record.

Howe also served as a role model for young hockey players. One of those players was future star Wayne Gretzky, who called Howe his "idol." Gretzky went on to break many of Howe's scoring records, but for all his greatness, even he knows there's only one "Mr. Hockey." That is Gordie Howe, the man who made hockey matter in the United States.

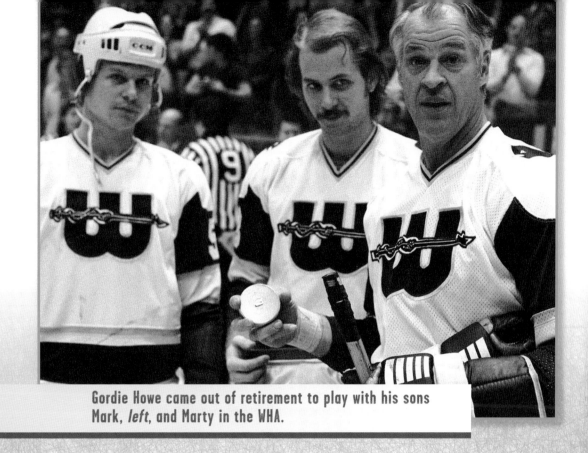

Gordie Howe came out of retirement to play with his sons Mark, *left*, and Marty in the WHA.

GORDIE HOWE

Hometown: Floral, Saskatchewan, Canada

Height, Weight: 6 feet, 205 pounds

Birth Date: March 31, 1928

Position: Right wing

Teams: Detroit Red Wings (1946–71), Houston Aeros (1973–77) (WHA), New England Whalers (1977–79) (WHA), Hartford Whalers (1979–80)

NHL All-Star Games: 23 (1948–55, 1957–65, 1967–71, 1980)

Hart Trophy (NHL MVP): 6 (1951–52, 1952–53, 1956–57, 1957–58, 1959–60, 1962–63)

All-NHL First Team: 12 (1950–51 through 1953–54, 1956–57, 1957–58, 1959–60, 1962–63, 1965–66, 1967–68 through 1969–70)

JACQUES PLANTE

Playing goaltender in hockey might be the toughest job in sports. Jacques Plante made sure it stopped being one of the scariest too.

Plante began his NHL career with the Montreal Canadiens in 1952. In those days, goalies did not wear masks. But that changed when Plante was hit in the face by a shot during a 1959 game. He went to the locker room for stitches. When he returned, he was wearing a mask for protection.

Montreal coach Toe Blake did not want Plante to wear the mask. But Plante refused to play otherwise. And the Canadiens did not have another goalie on the roster. So Plante wore the mask, and Montreal went on to win the game. The Canadiens then went on a long winning streak, and Plante never played another game without the mask.

Jacques Plante was a top NHL goaltender for more than 20 years.

The mask did more than keep Plante from getting hurt. It also made him more fearless on the ice. Plante was already the best goaltender in the world. When he put on the mask, he was even better. Plante spent 11 years in Montreal as the last line of defense for some of hockey's greatest teams. He led the Canadiens to a record five straight Stanley Cups.

During his career, Plante did more than just make playing goalie safer. He changed the way the position was played. Most goalies sat deep in the crease and waited for the shot. Plante, however, skated out toward an attacker to cut down the shooting angle. That made it tougher to find space to get the puck by him.

And when opponents tried to get the puck near Plante's face to scare him, it no longer worked. The NHL's first goaltending star had already taken care of that.

7

The number of Vezina Trophies, the award given each year to the NHL's top goaltender, Jacques Plante won during his career. That was still a record through 2014.

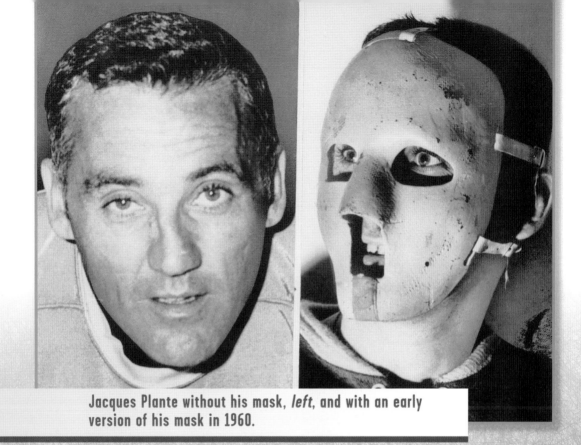

Jacques Plante without his mask, *left*, and with an early version of his mask in 1960.

JACQUES PLANTE

Hometown: Shawinigan Falls, Quebec, Canada

Height, Weight: 6 feet, 175 pounds

Birth Date: January 17, 1929

Position: Goaltender

Teams: Montreal Canadiens (1952–63), New York Rangers (1963–65), St. Louis Blues (1968–70), Toronto Maple Leafs (1970–73), Boston Bruins (1973), Edmonton Oilers (WHA) (1974–75)

NHL All-Star Games: 8 (1956–60, 1962, 1969, 1970)

Vezina Trophy (NHL Best Goaltender): 7 (1955–56 through 1959–60, 1961–62, 1968–69)

Hart Trophy (NHL MVP): 1 (1961–62)

All-NHL First Team: 3 (1955–56, 1958–59, 1961–62)

PHIL ESPOSITO

The Chicago Blackhawks were loaded with talent in the late 1960s. They were so loaded, in fact, that they felt they did not need promising young forward Phil Esposito. So the Blackhawks traded Esposito to the Boston Bruins in 1967. The six-player swap turned out to be one of the most one-sided trades in NHL history. Five of the players involved in the trade had decent careers. But Esposito went on to become one of the greatest scorers of all time.

Esposito was big enough to stand in front of the net and pound home rebounds. But he also had the soft hands and vision to thread passes through traffic to his teammates.

Esposito became the first player to ever score 100 points in an NHL season when he totaled 126 in 1968–69. And he was just getting started.

Phil Esposito helped lead the Boston Bruins to two Stanley Cup titles in the early 1970s.

Esposito topped 100 points five more times during the 1970s. He set a record with 152 points in 1970–71. That total included an amazing 76 goals.

Esposito and fellow Hall of Fame teammate Bobby Orr powered the Bruins to a pair of Stanley Cups in 1970 and 1972. But Esposito's finest moment may have come while playing for his home country in the 1972 Summit Series. That was a group of games pitting Canada against the Soviet Union.

The teams entered Game 8 with three wins, three losses, and one tie apiece. Whoever won Game 8 would take the series. That night, Esposito took over. He had four points in the game, including the assist on Paul Henderson's game-winning goal with 34 seconds left.

His teammates called Esposito's game his "finest hour." It was one of hockey's finest hours too.

717

The number of career goals Phil Esposito scored, ranking him fifth in NHL history through 2014.

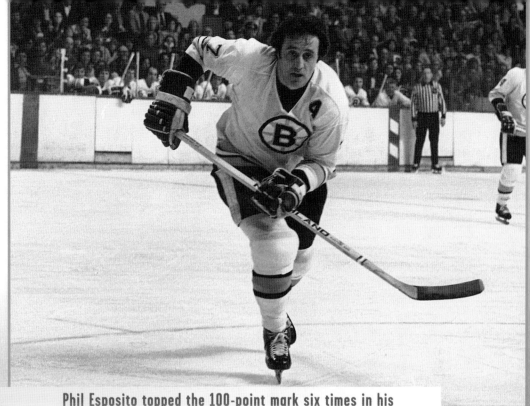

Phil Esposito topped the 100-point mark six times in his NHL career.

PHIL ESPOSITO

Hometown: Sault Ste. Marie, Ontario, Canada

Height, Weight: 6 feet 1, 205 pounds

Birth Date: February 20, 1942

Position: Center

Teams: Chicago Blackhawks (1963–67), Boston Bruins (1967–75), New York Rangers (1975–81)

NHL All-Star Games: 10 (1969–75, 1977, 1978, 1980)

Hart Trophy (NHL MVP): 2 (1968–69, 1973–74)

All-NHL First Team: 6 (1968–69 through 1973–74)

BOBBY ORR

Bobby Orr was flying. At least, it looked like he was. Orr's Boston Bruins and the visiting St. Louis Blues were tied in overtime of Game 4 of the 1970 Stanley Cup Finals. Orr took a pass along the boards and raced toward the St. Louis goal. He was in front of Blues goaltender Glenn Hall when St. Louis defenseman Noel Picard tripped him.

Picard's ploy worked. But it did not stop Orr from making history.

Not only did Orr get a shot off, he beat Hall to give the Bruins the victory and the Cup. Orr celebrated while he was still in midair. The picture of Orr parallel to the ice is one of the most famous in hockey history.

Bobby Orr flies through the air after scoring the Stanley Cup-clinching goal in 1970.

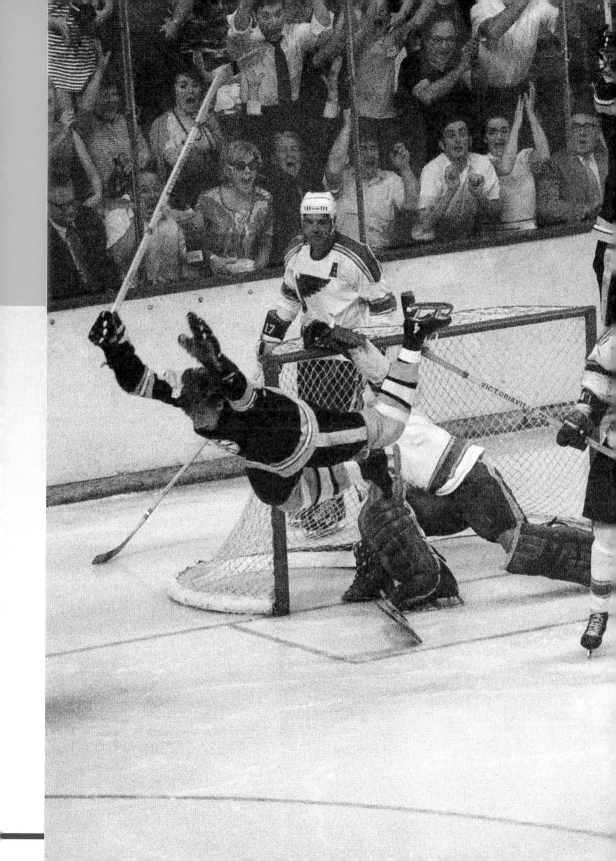

That play summed up Orr's remarkable career. He seemed to have only one speed: as fast as he could go. That speed made him one of the best defenseman in NHL history. Orr could race up the ice to help out the offense. And he did that well enough to lead the NHL in scoring twice. Yet he was also quick enough to get back on defense when the puck came back the other way.

Orr won the Norris Trophy as the NHL's top defenseman eight straight times between 1968 and 1975. He likely would have added to that total if not for a left knee injury that never seemed to heal. Orr retired in 1978 at the age of 30, ending a short career that lasted just over a decade.

102

The number of assists Bobby Orr had during the 1970–71 season, which was still a record for a defenseman through 2014.

But even in such a short time, Bobby Orr's exciting play provided memories for a lifetime.

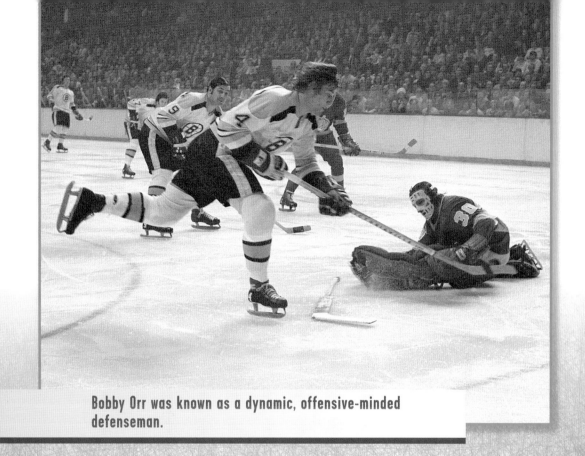

Bobby Orr was known as a dynamic, offensive-minded defenseman.

BOBBY ORR

Hometown: Parry Sound, Ontario, Canada

Height, Weight: 6 feet, 197 pounds

Birth Date: March 20, 1948

Position: Defense

Teams: Boston Bruins (1966–76), Chicago Blackhawks (1976–79)

NHL All-Star Games: 7 (1968–73, 1975)

Calder Trophy (NHL Rookie of the Year): 1966–67

Hart Trophy (NHL MVP): 3 (1969–70 through 1971–72)

Norris Trophy (NHL Top Defenseman): 8 (1967–68 through 1974-75)

Conn Smythe Trophy (Playoff MVP): 2 (1970, 1972)

All-NHL First Team: 8 (1967–68 through 1974–75)

GUY LAFLEUR

Hockey is not usually known for its beauty. Yet there was something about the way Guy Lafleur played that made it seem graceful. Perhaps it was his long blond hair. Most players did not wear helmets in Lafleur's era. So whenever he would race up the ice, his hair appeared to flow behind him in slow motion. At times, it seemed as if his opponents were doing the same thing. It was almost impossible to catch the man they called "The Flower."

Lafleur's elegant style was his trademark in Montreal, where he played most of his 17-year career. Wearing the blue-and-red Canadiens sweater, Lafleur was the face of a team that dominated the 1970s.

Guy Lafleur was one of the most graceful players in NHL history.

Lafleur led the NHL in scoring three times. He poured in a career-high 60 goals in 1977–78. But he saved his best hockey for the playoffs. Montreal won five Stanley Cups with Lafleur on the ice. That includes four straight from 1976 through 1979. He led or was tied for the team lead in scoring in each of those playoff runs. He also won the Conn Smythe Trophy, given to the MVP of the postseason, in 1977.

Lafleur was so good for so long that he racked up a lot of great moments. So when the Canadiens were thinking of a way to honor him after his retirement in 1991, they did not choose a famous play. Instead, they chose a famous image. Outside the Bell Centre, where the Canadiens play their home games, is a statue of Lafleur. He is posed with a stick in his hands, his hair flaring out behind him, and a goal in his sights.

1,246

The number of career points Guy Lafleur had, which was still the most in Canadiens history through 2014.

Guy Lafleur led the Montreal Canadiens to five Stanley Cups in the 1970s.

GUY LAFLEUR

Hometown: Thurso, Quebec, Canada

Height, Weight: 6 feet, 185 pounds

Birth Date: September 20, 1951

Position: Right wing

Teams: Montreal Canadiens (1971–85), New York Rangers (1988–89), Quebec Nordiques (1989–91)

NHL All-Star Games: 6 (1975–78, 1980, 1991)

Hart Trophy (NHL MVP): 2 (1976–77, 1977–78)

Conn Smythe Trophy (Playoff MVP): 1 (1976–77)

All-NHL First Team: 6 (1974–75 through 1979–80)

WAYNE GRETZKY

Walter Gretzky grew tired of taking his six-year-old son, Wayne, to a local park to practice hockey. So Walter built a rink in the family's backyard. That way Walter could watch from inside the house as Wayne worked on his skills. Given the chance to skate whenever he wanted, Wayne became more than just a good player. He became "The Great One."

By age 14, Wayne Gretzky was one of the most famous hockey players in the world. By age 20, he was setting NHL records that will likely never be broken. By the time he retired in 1999 after 21 seasons, No. 99 was a legend.

Gretzky won the Hart Trophy with the Edmonton Oilers in 1980. He remained the only first-year player to do so through 2014. And it was the first of many firsts for the smooth-skating center.

Wayne Gretzky celebrates scoring his 1,851st career point, breaking Gordie Howe's NHL record in 1989.

There have been fast players. There have been smart players. There have been strong players. No player before or since, though, had the combination of all three skills quite like Gretzky.

Gretzky scored a record 92 goals and finished with 212 points in 1981–82. That was the first of four seasons Gretzky topped the 200-point barrier. No other player had done it even once through 2014.

Gretzky led the Edmonton Oilers to four Stanley Cups in the 1980s. He then helped spread the NHL's popularity in the United States. The Oilers traded Gretzky to the Los Angeles Kings in 1988. He spent the final decade of his career playing in the United States. During that time, the NHL expanded to such warm-weather cities as Miami, Tampa, Anaheim, and Nashville. Those new fans got a chance to see "The Great One" and discovered why hockey was so popular elsewhere.

8

The number of consecutive years Wayne Gretzky won the Hart Memorial Trophy as the NHL's MVP. No other player had won the award more than three straight times through 2014.

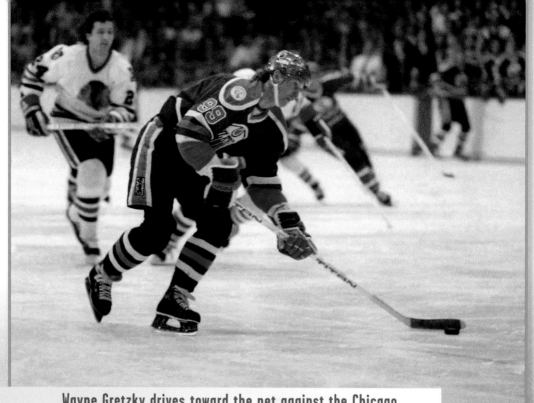

Wayne Gretzky drives toward the net against the Chicago Blackhawks in 1983.

WAYNE GRETZKY

Hometown: Brantford, Ontario, Canada

Height, Weight: 6 feet, 185 pounds

Birth Date: January 26, 1961

Position: Center

Teams: Indianapolis Racers (1978–79) (WHA), Edmonton Oilers (1979–88), Los Angeles Kings (1988–96), St. Louis Blues (1996), New York Rangers (1996–99)

NHL All-Star Games: 18 (1980–86, 1988–94, 1996–99)

Hart Trophy (NHL MVP): 9 (1979–80 through 1986–87, 1988–89)

Conn Smythe Trophy (Playoff MVP): 2 (1984–85, 1987–88)

All-NHL First Team: 8 (1980–81 through 1986–87, 1990–91)

Olympic Appearances: 1 (1998)

MARK MESSIER

The New York Rangers needed a spark. One more loss to the New Jersey Devils in the 1994 Eastern Conference finals would end New York's season.

Mark Messier had an idea. The Rangers' gritty captain decided it was time to do something bold. Heading into Game 6 in New Jersey, Messier told reporters the Rangers would win. He was trying to take the pressure off his teammates. Instead, all it did was make them mad. They were not sure promising victory was a good idea.

Messier delivered anyway. He scored three goals in the third period as New York rallied to beat the Devils 4–2. The Rangers went on to win the series. Then they beat the Vancouver Canucks in the Stanley Cup Finals for their first championship since 1940.

Mark Messier, *left*, hoists the Stanley Cup with Edmonton Oilers teammate Wayne Gretzky in 1988.

As the team captain, Messier was the first Ranger to touch the Cup in celebration. It might have been the sweetest of the six Stanley Cups he captured during his 26-year professional career. That is because it was the one that thrust him into the spotlight.

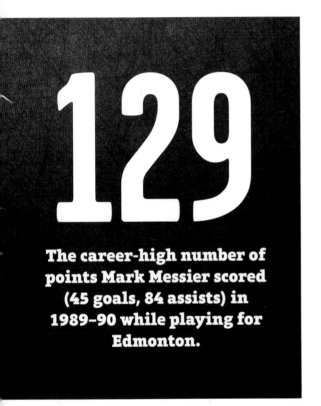

129

The career-high number of points Mark Messier scored (45 goals, 84 assists) in 1989–90 while playing for Edmonton.

During his early playing days, Messier played alongside Wayne Gretzky with the Edmonton Oilers. While Messier was a great player, Gretzky was a superstar. Eventually "The Great One" moved on. The Oilers were still plenty strong, but people wondered if Messier could win without Gretzky. When he captained the Oilers to the Cup in 1990 and the Rangers to the Cup in 1994, he answered that question.

By the time Messier retired in 2005 at age 44, he was the second-leading scorer in NHL history. Messier piled up 1,887 career points, including 694 goals.

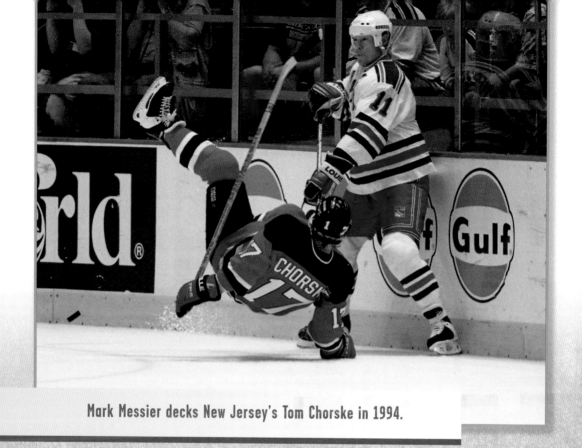

Mark Messier decks New Jersey's Tom Chorske in 1994.

MARK MESSIER

Hometown: Edmonton, Alberta, Canada

Height, Weight: 6 feet 1, 210 pounds

Birth Date: January 18, 1961

Position: Center/Left wing

Teams: Indianapolis Racers (1978–79) (WHA), Cincinnati Stingers (1978–79) (WHA), Edmonton Oilers (1979–91), New York Rangers (1991–97, 2000–04), Vancouver Canucks (1997–2000)

NHL All-Star Games: 15 (1982–84, 1986, 1988–92, 1994, 1996–98, 2000, 2004)

Hart Trophy (NHL MVP): 2 (1989–90, 1991–92)

Conn Smythe Award (Playoff MVP): 1 (1983–84)

All-NHL First Team: 4 (1981–82, 1982–83, 1989–90, 1991–92)

RAY
BOURQUE

Ray Bourque could not breathe. He wanted to cry. But the game was not even over yet. So Bourque held off the tears until the horn sounded in Game 7 of the 2001 Stanley Cup Finals. That is when the tears started streaming onto Bourque's beard. After 21 years of searching, one of the greatest defenseman in NHL history was finally a champion.

When NHL commissioner Gary Bettman handed the Cup to Joe Sakic, the Colorado Avalanche captain did not take off with it. Instead he handed it to Bourque, even though Bourque had only been with the team for a little more than a year.

"He's the one that deserved to lift it up first," Sakic said.

Ray Bourque celebrates after finally winning the Stanley Cup with the Colorado Avalanche in 2001.

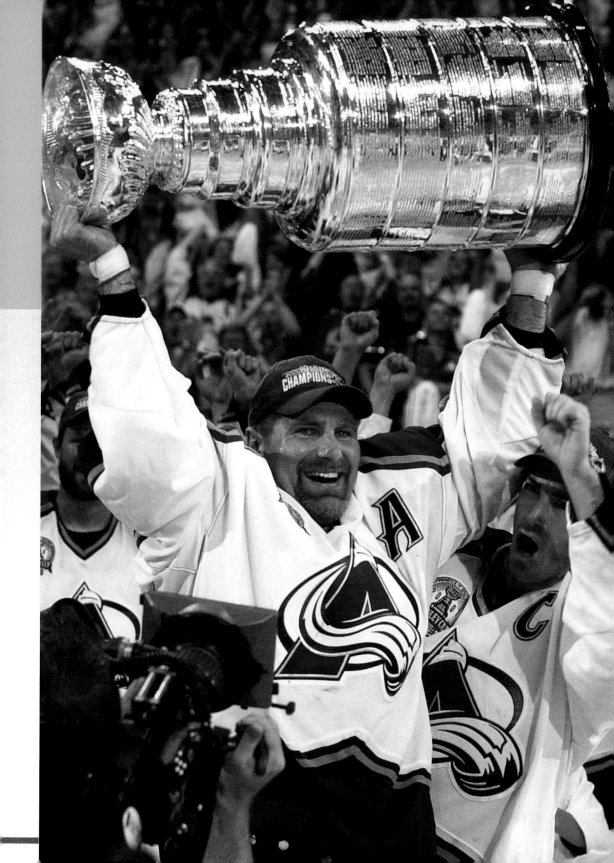

Bourque spent the first 20 and a half years of his career with the Boston Bruins. He built a reputation as a talented scorer and a tough defender. He won the Norris Trophy five times. And he missed the All-Star Game just twice during his career.

1,506

Ray Bourque's point total (395 goals, 1,111 assists) during his time with the Bruins, which was still a team record through 2014.

The only thing that Bourque did not win with the Bruins was the one thing that mattered the most: the Cup. Boston came close in 1988 and 1990, only to lose to Edmonton in the finals. It was hard to blame Bourque for the loss. He was Boston's best player during both playoff runs.

The Bruins were struggling in the late 1990s when they decided to do Bourque a favor. They traded him to Colorado, one of the NHL's best teams, late in the 1999–2000 season. A little more than a year later, the moment Bourque was waiting for finally arrived. The Avalanche won the Cup. So did the player who had spent so long searching for hockey's biggest prize.

Ray Bourque was a standout defenseman for the Boston Bruins for 21 seasons.

RAY BOURQUE

Hometown: Montreal, Quebec, Canada

Height, Weight: 5 feet 11, 219 pounds

Birth Date: December 28, 1960

Position: Defense

Teams: Boston Bruins (1979–2000), Colorado Avalanche (2000–01)

NHL All-Star Games: 19 (1981–86, 1988–94, 1996–2001)

Calder Trophy (NHL Top Rookie): 1979–80

Norris Trophy (NHL Top Defenseman): 5 (1986–87, 1987–88, 1989–90, 1990–91, 1993–94)

All-NHL First Team: 13 (1979–80, 1981–82, 1983–84, 1984–85, 1986–87, 1987–88, 1989–90 through 1993–94, 1995–96, 2000–01)

Olympic Appearances: 1 (1998)

MARIO LEMIEUX

Mario Lemieux won two Stanley Cups during his time with the Pittsburgh Penguins. "Super Mario" made hockey look as easy as playing a video game. His greatest achievement, however, might have come off the ice.

In 1993, Lemieux found out he had a form of cancer called Hodgkin's disease. He needed to take some time off to undergo treatment. He spent some time away from the game hoping to recover. Two months after telling his teammates he was sick, Lemieux returned to the Penguins. As usual, he made a grand entrance. He scored a goal and picked up an assist in his first game back. Even the fans of the rival Philadelphia Flyers cheered for Lemieux.

"Super Mario" was back.

Mario Lemieux was a magician with the puck on his stick.

It seemed for much of his career, Lemieux's biggest opponent was not the other team. It was his body. When healthy, Lemieux was nearly unstoppable. He was often the biggest and the fastest player on the ice. And he could make magic happen with his stick.

1.88

The number of points per game Mario Lemieux averaged during his career. That was second all-time behind Wayne Gretzky through 2014.

Lemieux led the NHL in scoring six times during his career. That number could have been much higher if he could have stayed on the ice. But back problems forced him to miss the 1994–95 season and led to an early retirement in 1997. He was immediately inducted into the Hockey Hall of Fame.

But three years later, "Super Mario" returned to the Penguins. He won a gold medal with Canada in the 2002 Olympic Winter Games. Lemieux retired for good in 2006 with 1,723 career points. He did not go far away from the game, though. Lemieux led a group that bought the Penguins in 1999, and he stayed on as team owner after his playing days ended.

Flashy moves and keen vision made "Super Mario" a nightmare for defenders.

MARIO LEMIEUX

Hometown: Montreal, Quebec, Canada

Height, Weight: 6 feet 4, 230 pounds

Birth Date: October 5, 1965

Position: Center

Team: Pittsburgh Penguins (1984–97, 2000–06)

Calder Trophy (NHL Top Rookie): 1984-85

NHL All-Star Games: 10 (1985, 1986, 1988–90, 1992, 1996, 1997, 2001, 2002)

Hart Trophy (NHL MVP): 3 (1987–88, 1992–93, 1995–96)

Conn Smythe Trophy (Playoff MVP): 2 (1990–91, 1991–92)

All-NHL First Team: 5 (1987–88, 1988–89, 1992–93, 1995–96, 1996–97)

Olympic Appearances: 1 (2002, gold)

NICKLAS LIDSTROM

Nicklas Lidstrom stood near the blue line and waited. A moment later, the puck was on his stick. With one swing of his arms, the defenseman let loose a slap shot that looked like a blur as it zipped past the goalie.

Of all the goals Lidstrom scored in his long hockey career, this one was the biggest. It came in the third period of the gold-medal game at the 2006 Olympic Winter Games. And it gave Sweden a 3–2 victory over Finland.

It is fitting that Lidstrom played the hero. For years the soft-spoken star had been paving the way in the NHL for other hockey players born outside North America.

Nicklas Lidstrom celebrates after scoring the gold-medal-winning goal for Sweden at the 2006 Winter Olympics.

The Detroit Red Wings picked Lidstrom in the third round of the 1989 draft. He made his NHL debut in 1991. Lidstrom then spent all 20 seasons of his NHL career with the Red Wings. For two decades, he was the anchor for one of hockey's best teams.

1,564

The number of games Nicklas Lidstrom played with the Red Wings—the most by a player who spent his entire career with one team.

While he could score goals with that booming slap shot, Lidstrom's greatest strength was his intelligence. He knew what opponents liked to do when they were near the Detroit net. And he usually knew how to stop them.

Lidstrom was not very big. But he made up for it with his skating. He was so smooth that it looked as if he were gliding up and down the ice. Red Wings teammate Steve Yzerman said Lidstrom made everyone else's job easier. Then again, Lidstrom had a habit of making everything look easy—especially winning.

A stalwart defenseman, Lidstrom also was famous for his blistering slap shot.

NICKLAS LIDSTROM

Hometown: Vasteras, Sweden

Height, Weight: 6 feet 1, 192 pounds

Birth Date: April 28, 1970

Position: Defense

Team: Detroit Red Wings (1991–2012)

NHL All-Star Games: 11 (1996, 1998–2004, 2007, 2008, 2011)

Norris Trophy (NHL Top Defenseman): 7 (2000–01 through 2003–04, 2006–07, 2007–08, 2010–11)

Conn Smythe Trophy (Playoff MVP): 1 (2001–02)

All-NHL First Team: 10 (1997–98 through 2002–03, 2005–06 through 2007–08, 2010–11)

Olympic Appearances: 4 (1998, 2002, 2006 gold, 2010)

MARTIN BRODEUR

Martin Brodeur had a decision to make. Growing up in Canada, Brodeur was a pretty good forward. But he could play goaltender too. When he was seven years old, his coach asked him to make a choice.

It turned out to be an easy one. Brodeur's father, Denis, was an outstanding goalie. He had helped Canada to a bronze medal in the 1956 Winter Olympics. Martin knew he wanted to follow his dad's path. But he ended up blazing a new trail.

The New Jersey Devils called Martin Brodeur up to the NHL in the spring of 1992. He was just 19. Yet he played like someone a decade older. Goaltenders are not known for being calm, but Brodeur never seemed rattled. Whether he made a spectacular save or was beaten for a goal, he kept his emotions in check.

Martin Brodeur was rock solid in the net for the New Jersey Devils.

Brodeur's confidence carried over to his teammates. He was just 22 when he led the Devils on an unlikely run to the Stanley Cup. He went 16–4 in the playoffs, allowing less than two goals per game. It marked the start of a long run of success for both the Devils and their steady goaltender. New Jersey won it all again in 2000 and 2003. Brodeur looked like a brick wall wearing a No. 30 jersey.

Brodeur did not have to make many flashy saves. He had a knack for putting his body into perfect position so opponents had nothing to shoot at when they came his way. Playing that way helped Brodeur stay healthy and pick up win after win. By the end of the 2013–14 season, he held every major NHL goaltending record. Among them were career victories (688), shutouts (124), and games played (1,259).

31,540

The number of shots Martin Brodeur had faced through the end of the 2013–14 season—the most in league history.

Martin Brodeur was the man in the middle for Canada in the 2010 Winter Olympics.

MARTIN BRODEUR

Hometown: Montreal, Quebec, Canada

Height, Weight: 6 feet 2, 220 pounds

Birth Date: May 6, 1972

Position: Goaltender

Team: New Jersey Devils (1991–)

NHL All-Star Games: 9 (1996–2001, 2003, 2004, 2007)

Calder Trophy (NHL Top Rookie): 1993–94

Vezina Trophy (NHL Top Goaltender): 4 (2002–03, 2003–04, 2006–07, 2007–08)

All-NHL First Team: 3 (2002–03, 2003–04, 2006–07)

Olympic Appearances: 4 (1998, 2002 gold, 2006, 2010 gold)

HAYLEY WICKENHEISER

Hayley Wickenheiser received a pair of figure skates when she was three years old. The figure skates didn't last long.

Wickenheiser didn't want to glide across the ice and gracefully fly through the air. She wanted a hockey stick and a puck. And she wanted the kind of skates that would power her from one end of the rink to the other faster than anybody else.

So her father, Tom, went out and purchased a pair of hockey skates, even though girls didn't play much hockey back in the 1980s.

With the proper skates on her feet, the game came easy to Wickenheiser. Her rise came at a time when the women's game was starting to spread. She was named to the Canadian national team at age 15 and was only 19 when she was named to the first Canadian women's Olympic hockey team in 1998.

Hayley Wickenheiser celebrates a goal at the 2014 Winter Olympics in Sochi, Russia.

In Wickenheiser's first Olympics, Canada fell to the United States in the gold medal game in Nagano, Japan. She and her teammates won every other Olympic gold medal through 2014.

She was still going strong at the 2014 games in Sochi, Russia. She drew a key penalty in the gold medal game against Team USA to help Canada to its fourth straight Olympic title.

Wickenheiser made history in 2003 when she scored while playing in a men's league in Finland. She later spent an entire season playing with men in a Swedish league in 2008–09.

Her success has made her a hero in her homeland. Wickenheiser carried the Canadian flag during the Opening Ceremony at the 2014 Winter Games. She was given the Order of Canada, the second-highest honor a Canadian citizen can receive, for her role in helping women's hockey escape from the shadow of the men's game.

2

The number of women who have competed for Canada in both the Summer and Winter Olympics. Wickenheiser is one. She played softball in the 2000 Summer Games.

Hayley Wickenheiser celebrates a goal against Team USA at the 2014 Winter Olympics.

HAYLEY WICKENHEISER

Hometown: Shaunavon, Saskatchewan, Canada

Height, Weight: 5 feet 10, 180 pounds

Birth Date: August 12, 1978

Position: Forward

Olympic Appearances: 5 (1998 silver, 2002 gold, 2006 gold, 2010 gold, 2014 gold)

SIDNEY CROSBY

Sidney Crosby saw Jarome Iginla go into the corner with the puck, so he shouted "Iggy!" Canadian teammate Iginla sent a pass to a streaking Crosby. With a flick of the wrist, "Sid the Kid" joined Canadian hockey royalty.

Crosby's overtime goal vaulted Canada to victory over Team USA in the gold-medal game of the 2010 Winter Olympics. The moment was even sweeter because it came on home ice in Vancouver, Canada. Crosby was mobbed by his teammates while Canadian citizens took to the streets in joy.

"That kid is Hockey Canada," said US player Tim Gleason. "It was almost like a too-good-to-be-true story that he scored the goal."

Sidney Crosby was named captain of the Pittsburgh Penguins at age 19.

Crosby's golden goal was the final step in a march that had begun almost at birth. Like his role model Wayne Gretzky, Crosby became famous for his talent as a teenager. The Pittsburgh Penguins chose him with the first pick in the 2005 draft. The Penguins were among the worst teams in the NHL when Crosby arrived. But that changed quickly.

Crosby was named team captain at age 19. The Penguins built themselves into an NHL power thanks to Crosby's tireless work. Not the biggest, fastest, or strongest player, Crosby became one of the best by working harder than anyone else. He wore down his opponents.

So did the Penguins. Pittsburgh won the Stanley Cup in 2009 with Crosby leading the way. And in 2013–14, Crosby came back from serious concussion problems to win his second league MVP Award and second Olympic gold medal.

120

Sidney Crosby's career-high point total (36 goals, 84 assists) during the 2006–07 season, giving him the first of two NHL scoring titles through 2014.

Sidney Crosby beats US goalie Ryan Miller in overtime to win the gold medal game at the 2010 Winter Olympics.

SIDNEY CROSBY

Hometown: Cole Harbour, Nova Scotia, Canada

Height, Weight: 5 feet 11, 200 pounds

Birth Date: August 7, 1987

Position: Center

Team: Pittsburgh Penguins (2006–)

NHL All-Star Games: 1 (2007)

Hart Trophy (NHL MVP): 2 (2006–07, 2013–14)

First-Team All-NHL: 3 (2006–07, 2012–13, 2013–14)

Olympic Appearances: 2 (2010 gold, 2014 gold)

HONORABLE MENTIONS

Paul Coffey – One of the best offensive defensemen ever, Coffey won the Norris Trophy three times as the NHL's top defenseman during a 21-year career that ended in 2001.

Ron Francis – The NHL's fourth all-time leading scorer, Francis was a two-time Stanley Cup champion while playing for the Pittsburgh Penguins in the 1990s.

Cammi Granato – Granato was the captain of the US squad that won the first gold medal in Olympic women's hockey in 1998. She was inducted into the Hockey Hall of Fame in 2010.

Dominik Hasek – The six-time Vezina Trophy winner as the NHL's top goaltender also won the Hart Trophy as the NHL's MVP in 1997 and 1998 while playing for the Buffalo Sabres.

Brett Hull – Hull was the third-leading goal scorer in NHL history and one of the top US players of all time. He won the 1999 and 2002 Stanley Cups and one Hart Trophy during his 20-year career.

Angela James – The Canadian was called the Wayne Gretzky of women's hockey for her exciting play. She was elected to the Hockey Hall of Fame in 2010.

Patrick Roy – Roy won three Vezina Trophies as the NHL's top goaltender in the 1980s and 1990s. He also won four Stanley Cups and three Conn Smythe Trophies as the playoff MVP.

Angela Ruggiero – A star defenseman for Team USA in four Olympics, Ruggiero helped the Americans win one gold, two silver, and one bronze medal between 1998 and 2010.

Vladislav Tretiak – The Russian goalie powered the Soviet Union to three Olympic gold medals in 1972, 1976, and 1984.

Steve Yzerman – Yzerman is a three-time Stanley Cup champion and was sixth all-time in NHL career points through 2014. His career, which lasted from 1983 to 2006, is considered one of the best ever for a two-way forward.

GLOSSARY

archrival
The opposing team that brings out the greatest emotion from fans and players.

assist
A pass to a teammate that results in a goal scored.

captain
The team leader and the only player allowed to speak to game officials regarding the rules.

check
An intentional collision between two players on different teams.

overtime
The time added to the end of a game if no winner is decided during regulation time.

power play
When a team has more players on the ice than the opponent because of the opponent's penalties.

shutout
When one team does not score any goals in a game.

slap shot
A shot in which the player raises the stick and swings downward, hitting the puck for more power and speed.

FOR MORE INFORMATION

Further Readings

Peters, Chris. *Stanley Cup Finals*. Minneapolis, MN: Abdo Publishing, 2013.

Weisman, Blaine and Leia Tait. *Hockey (Record Breakers Series)*. New York, NY: Weigl Publishers Inc., 2010.

Zweig, Eric. *Super Scorers*. Richmond Hill, Ontario, Canada: Firefly Books, 2014.

Websites

To learn more about Sports' Best Ever, visit **booklinks.abdopublishing.com**. These links are routinely monitored and updated to provide the most current information available.

INDEX

ABOUT THE AUTHOR

Will Graves caught the hockey bug while watching the Washington Capitals in the 1980s. He turned out to be better at writing about goals than scoring them. He currently is a sportswriter for the Associated Press in Pittsburgh, where he covers the NFL, MLB, and NHL, focusing on the Pittsburgh Penguins. He has also covered three Olympic Games for the AP.